HEY-HO
WHAT A SUMMER

JANE MARRINER

AuthorHouse™ UK
1663 Liberty Drive
Bloomington, IN 47403 USA
www.authorhouse.co.uk
UK TFN: 0800 0148641 (Toll Free inside the UK)
UK Local: 02036 956322 (+44 20 3695 6322 from outside the UK)

Because of the dynamic nature of the Internet, any web addresses or links contained in this book may have changed since publication and may no longer be valid. The views expressed in this work are solely those of the author and do not necessarily reflect the views of the publisher, and the publisher hereby disclaims any responsibility for them.

This book is printed on acid-free paper.

ISBN: 979-8-8230-8365-2 (sc)
ISBN: 979-8-8230-8366-9 (e)

Library of Congress Control Number: 2023912924

Print information available on the last page.

Published by AuthorHouse 07/13/2023

authorHOUSE

HEY-HO
WHAT A SUMMER

Paddy and Petunia lived in a pretty little thatched cottage just outside the village where Petunia tended to her front garden filled with summer flowers. Custard Cat who only ate custard and his friend Ming Mouse who only ate cheese, also lived in the cottage.

There was a paddock adjoining the cottage with a large barn. Paddy covered the floor of the barn with fresh hay for Hay-Neigh Horse, Dinky-Donk Donkey and Guzzle Goat to sleep on at night. Hay-Neigh Horse sported a cap and a cane. Dinky-Donk Donkey wore a bow-tie and Guzzle Goat a tail hoop.

There was a pond in the paddock where Giddy-Blue Goose loved to swim in ever decreasing circles. This upset Freddy Frog's concentration, as he liked to sit on a rock in the pond with mouth agape. He kept a tally of all the flying insects he could catch in this way. However, Freddy Frog could never catch Fuzz-Buzz Fly who enjoyed landing on everyone's nose, tickling them and making them sneeze.

Henrik Hedgehog lived in the bushes at the edge of the paddock with his hedgehog family. Whilst seeking out food for dinner, Henrik Hedgehog would be gently tupped from behind by his friend Guzzle Goat with his curly horns. Guzzle Goat was always hungry but Henrik Hedgehog failed to tempt him with the worms, slugs and snails he had collected.

Their neighbour, Sarah-Lou often visited with Dilly-Dally Dolly, and together they were given rides by Dinky-Donk Donkey who proudly trotted round the paddock with his head held high.

Victor the Vet lived in the heart of the village above his small surgery, where he looked after all the poorly animals and birds until they were well enough to return home.

Victor the Vet was also a farrier and kept a forge behind the surgery where he made new metal shoes for all the village horses. Hay-Neigh Horse loved to talk to Victor the Vet whilst being fitted with new shoes which Victor the Vet dipped in red metallic paint, just for him. "I am the only horse in the County with bright red horse shoes!" boasted Hay-Neigh Horse. He delighted in taking the old worn shoes home where he hung them up in the barn for decoration.

On one visit, Victor the Vet seemed very sad. "I need more room for all my poorly patients," he sighed. "I must look for somewhere with much greater space."

Back in the paddock, Dinky-Donk Donkey was giving Sarah-Lou and Dilly-Dally Dolly their usual ride. Suddenly, Fuzz-Buzz Fly flew onto Dinky-Donks's nose and made him sneeze so violently that Dilly-Dally Dolly was thrown high in the air. She disappeared in the bushes at the edge of the paddock. Everyone looked for her but Dilly-Dally Dolly couldn't be found.

etunia ran back to the cottage and returned with Bonnie Bear.

"My granddaughter left Bonnie Bear when she last visited, so I will give her to you, Sarah-Lou. I know you will love her, and she will be a friend for Dilly-Dally Dolly when she returns." said Petunia.

In a corner of the paddock, Henrik Hedgehog helped Dilly-Dally Dolly to her feet and invited her for a cup of herbal hedgehog tea. The hedgehog family were talking to two flowers sitting beside them.

"We always enjoy a Summer Flower Ball" explained the flowers, "and Petunia bakes cakes and biscuits to eat in the paddock."

"That sounds lovely" said Dilly-Dally Dolly, who offered to stay and help.

Later, Paddy and Petunia told everyone that they had decided to move to the seaside to live near their daughter and grandchildren "and to grow another flower garden" added Petunia.

"We will find someone to take over the cottage and the paddock. They will look after you all", promised Paddy.

However, word had spread that Paddy and Petunia wanted to move. Shortly afterwards, three people arrived at Paddy and Petunia's cottage.

There was Mauve Man who was a mauve colour from head to toe. With him came Lanky Lad carrying a clipboard wider than himself. Lastly, came Lottie Stiletto who could barely totter as the heels of her shoes were so high.

They outlined their plan to replace the cottage with a huge warehouse holding goods for distribution to shops around the country. The paddock was to be replaced by a wide road for carrying all the heavy goods vehicles used to collect and deliver to and from the warehouse.

A large picture window would display goods. These would include a glass fish, a spaceship, and a chocolate penguin. Also, a wheelbarrow full of dolls, a Christmas tree, and a carousel of miniature horses.

"This is terrible! Think of all the pollution, with fumes and grime from heavy vehicles spoiling our village" cried Paddy and Petunia.

"Are WE going to be put in the warehouse window?" spluttered Hay-Neigh Horse. "I am too big for that carousel!" he gasped in horror.

"If they put me next to that chocolate penguin, I shall EAT it"! Vowed Guzzle Goat.

"No one puts ME in a wheelbarrow", declared Dilly-Dally Dolly, who had now returned across the paddock.

"No! No! No!" everyone shouted in unison. They all looked at each other.

Then, Custard Cat poured a jugful of custard over Lanky Lad turning him buttercup yellow. Ming Mouse threw crumbs of cheese under Mauve Man's feet causing him to stumble down the cottage path. Guzzle Goat followed, poking him with his curly horns.

Lottie Stiletto tottered to the garden bench but found herself sitting on a row of sharp spined hedgehogs. Dilly-Dally Dolly tied her two plaits together and lassoed Lottie Stiletto, whose high heeled shoes fell off. Giddy-Blue Goose waddled away with one of them, hissing all the while.

Fuzz-Buzz Fly landed on Mauve Man's nose making him sneeze, and Freddy Frog croaked menacingly at the three of them.

Mauve Man, Lanky Lad and Lottie Stiletto somehow managed to stagger away to their car, abandoning their warehouse plan for ever.

It was decided that Victor the Vet would take over the cottage and run his surgery and forge from the barn. There was plenty of room for his poorly patients, and enough room for Hay-Neigh Horse, Dinky-Donk Donkey and Guzzle Goat to sleep inside at night. Sarah-Lou, Dilly-Dally Dolly and Bonnie Bear would continue to enjoy rides around the paddock.

Everyone celebrated with a wonderful Summer Flower Ball where Victor the Vet acted as Disc Jockey. Petunia's cakes and biscuits were eaten enthusiastically.

Next day, they all gathered to wave goodbye to Paddy, Petunia, Custard Cat and Ming Mouse.

Victor the Vet promised to look after the garden. Paddy and Petunia were looking forward to many visits, to see all the beautiful flowers, and to greet all their friends again.